# Hangin' With My Auntie!

by Sally North

Can't wait to see you again!

We have so much fun
hanging out together!

Hangin' with my auntie
is a special kind of fun.

# We do all kinds of crazy things...

like dancing in the sun!

Sometimes we do a handstand...

or just run around the park.

Or hide beneath the blankets...

when it's really, really dark.

Sometimes we
bake some cupcakes...

or some other yummy food.

We act a little silly...

# HAPPY

'cause we're in a happy mood!

Sometimes when
I'm at aunties place...

# I play with lots of toys.

And then she reads a book to me,
and I don't make a noise.

Sometimes we do some shopping at the big, amazing mall.

# Or play a little tennis...

or go play a little ball.

Then when it's time for me to leave,
she holds my hand so tight.

And says,
"Good-bye,
I love you,
see you later
and good night."

Hangin' With My Auntie!

Sally was born in Jackson, Michigan.  She has lived all over the country with her husband, Fred. They have 3 grown children, and they all live in Louisville, KY. She has written over 30 children's books and had her first book published in 2000.  Sneaky Snail Stories are all sweet and simple rhyming books with really cute illustrations.  You can see all the Sneaky Snail Stories at: www. sneakysnailstories.com
Other books by Sally:

No Pancakes for Puppy
Grandma and Grandpa Love Me
No Cookies for Kitty
My Aunt Loves Me
The Best Day


Emma's Hilarious Horse Book (personalized for boys or girls with cats, dogs, penguins or frogs)
Emma, the Super, Amazing, Awesome, Intelligent, Girly-Girl (personalized)
Noah the Basketball Star (personalized for several sports for boys or girls)
Noah's Very Own Cook Book (personalized for boys or girls)
Grandma and Grandpa Love Emma (personalized from any relative for boys or girls)
Emma Turns One! (personalized for boys or girls ages 1-6)        and many more....

website:  www.sneakysnailstories.com        facebook:  Sneaky Snail Stories
Etsy:  (search for) thesneakysnailstore        Amazon:  (search for) Sally Helmick North

The Best Day!

written and illustrated by Sally Helmick North

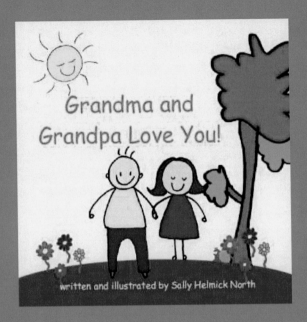

Grandma and Grandpa Love You!

written and illustrated by Sally Helmick North

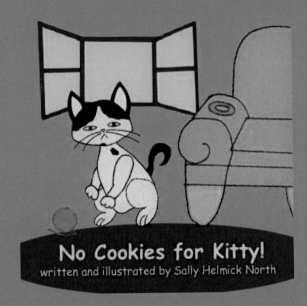

No Cookies for Kitty!

written and illustrated by Sally Helmick North

Your Aunt Loves You!

by Sally Helmick North